Henry Phillips

Volk-Songs

Henry Phillips

Volk-Songs

ISBN/EAN: 9783337020231

Printed in Europe, USA, Canada, Australia, Japan

Cover: Foto ©Andreas Hilbeck / pixelio.de

More available books at **www.hansebooks.com**

´ VOLK-SONGS

TRANSLATED FROM THE

ACTA COMPARATIONIS LITTERARUM UNIVERSARUM

BY

HENRY PHILLIPS Jr

.

——— ——

PHILADELPHIA
PRINTED FOR PRIVATE CIRCULATION
1885

PREFATORY NOTE.

THE originals from which these translations are made were gathered by the learned Dr. Hugo von Meltzel, of Kolozsvar, Hungary, and published by him in the *Összehasonlitó Irodalomtörténelmi Lapok* (*Acta Comparationis Litterarum Universarum*), a journal of great merit, of which he is the editor.

As they have never heretofore appeared in English, the translator ventures to present these studies of a popular mind.

Philadelphia,
    320 S. Eleventh St.

MAGYAR VOLK-SONGS.

I.

HALCYON joys are o'er me shed!
'Round my velvet hat so red
Winds a posy you may see
That my brown maid plucked for me.

Flowers culled she from the mead,
And I kissed her for the deed ;
Gather another for me, I pray,
And I'll hundred kisses pay.

" Baby mine, ope' wide thy door,
'Tis no Slav that stands before ;
'Tis a Magyar-born, I say—
Open—wherefore this delay?"

"Well enough I know thee now,
But I'll trust not to thy vow ;
Light of love, man is forsworn,
Turns away and laughs to scorn."

II.

I ne'er have robbed nor hurt my betters,
Yet here, conscripted, sit in fetters.

A huzzar's jacket fain I'd wear,
For now I trot on Shanks's mare.

Proud looks he from his charger's back,
When on the march, and smokes tabak.

The footman takes his weary way
Through miry morass, swamp and clay.

Loud oaths on guns and shoes resound
When in the marsh he's almost drowned.

And e'en the axe the butcher swung
Is cursed, that lamed the kid so young:

For since it means of motion lacks
The troops must bear it on their backs.

III.

Of what use is town or state
When a maid can find no mate?
Of what good this Puszta free—?
Barna Pista * loves not me.

What avail me jewels rare
If true love is absent there?
What the toil-full world if I
Like a flower must bloom and die?

* Brown Stephen.

What avails my slender waist
If no arm is 'round it placed?
What the starry heavens' glow
If my heart is fraught with woe?

Weeping at the dawn of day
For my sweetheart far away,
But *one* thing I fain would have,
Peace that waits me in the grave.

IV.

Golden life a maiden leads,
Lovers many watch her needs!
But the laddie—fie, for shame,—
Bloodhound-like hunts nightly game.

To their spinning maidens go
When the sunset's ceased to glow,
But the lad outside remains,
Peeping through the casement-panes.

As dull night the village shades
At their spinning sit the maids;
But the lover, luckless, bold,
To the window's frozen cold.

Frozen to the glass his lips,
Frozen to his finger tips! . . . . .

Quick, in pity, bring a light!
First, we'll thaw his mouth, poor wight!

V.

Tell me how to safely reach thee,
    Sweetest, dainty maid,
Lest through snarling of the mastiffs
    I should be betrayed?
"Each I'll throw a piece of meat,
They'll not bark, but silent eat,
    Then you'll safely come."

Tell me how to safely reach thee,
    Sweetest, dainty maid,
Lest through stabled steeds loud trampling
    I should be betrayed?
" Hay I'll strow before each eye,
They'll not move but quiet lie,
    Then you'll safely come."

Tell me how to safely reach thee,
    Sweetest, dainty maid,
Lest through cackling of the geeseyard
    I should be betrayed?
"Grain I'll spread before each beak,
Then no trumpet-note will speak,
    And you'll safely come."

Tell me how to safely reach thee,
    Sweetest, dainty maid,
Lest through Tom-cats' shrill mi–au–ing
    I should be betrayed?
"'Fore each cat some milk I'll place,
Then all noises they will cease,
    And you'll safely come."

Tell me how to safely reach thee,
    Dearest, dainty maid,
Lest through little mice's twittering
    I should be betrayed?
"Shame! thou hero! leave the house!
To be frightened at a mouse!
    Now, thou shalt not come!"

VI.

Wretched comrade, void of rest,
Always at the market guest,
Many a horse and cow I steal,
So I gain my daily meal.

Naught have I of any good,
But my body and young blood;
Were I only by my dove
Woe and pain would yield to love.

Naught care I if others weep,
Bread and butter let them keep ;
To the Tanya turn I free
Where my sweetheart waits for me.

Naught care I for treasure's store,
Jewels, diamonds, golden ore ;
Envy follows not my tread,
Danger threatens not my head.

When in earth I rest at last,
Fame and name forever past,
O'er my grave shall flowers spread,
Violets blue and roses red.

VII.

Poor, dear Berki ! who'll reply,
Why did poor, old Berki die ?
Wine enough they failed to give,
So friend Berki ceased to live.

Had they filled the glass in time
Berki died not in his prime ;
Ne'er a drop, not e'en the worst—
So our Berki died athirst.

Let no tongue e'er lisp his name,
Good friend Berki sleeps in fame ;

Let none seek the sickness dire
Through which Berki did expire.

Wine in time they failed to give,
So poor Berki ceased to live;
Had they filled the glass, I trow,
Berki would be living now.

VIII.

Though but sixteen years I bear
I'm a thief, expert in snare;
Steeds some thirty-three I stole,
Not a hoof betrayed my goal.

If the judge should cause me care,
Quick I'll loot a spanking pair;
Whilst I hide them out of sight,
Me to supper he'll invite.

In my purse is gold galore,
Gallant nags in plenteous store
In my stalls—not those I've stole'—
Swift they passed from my control.

But there's one, a dun-coat bright,
'With dark limbs o'er-flecked with white,
Who my form, 'twixt night and morn,
Pesth to Debrezin hath borne.

IX.

On no head should curse of God
Ever fall; but if the rod
Must descend, then may he pay
My assassin's deed to-day.

Where thou seek'st repose in shade
Withered trees shall fill the glade;
When thou'd fain in Csarda rest
May its fires consume thy breast!

Crops shall blight and vintage fail,
Insect hosts shall fields assail;
Both thy blades, so sharp and true,
Rend thy heart—and pierce it through.

X.

Now beneath this clan I fall;
And they bend me to their thrall;
Sorrow sore came with my wife,
No more pleasure's left in life.

Take good heed, my friend, to see
What your sweetheart's mother may be;
Should she be of evil kind—
All your days you'll bitter find!

XI.

" Broad the rolling Danube speeds,
Narrow bridge across it leads :
Dearest, heed thy steps, take care,
Lest thou slip in, unaware."

" Where the Donau's rapids brawl,
Never, never, shall I fall ;
But with you, my sweetest dove,
Must I tumble deep in love."

XII.

" Come, come, my prettie birdie ; just see the cage I
hold,
Here is a home I've built for thee, of purest, shining
gold ;
The golden casements glisten, the silver hinges clink,
From out of diamond basins, see, thou shalt eat and
drink !"

" No, no, I cannot dwell thus, in golden bonds re-
strained,
But in the merry greenwood must I roam, unchecked,
unchained ;
Where juniper is plenty, 'midst tender berries bright,
I quench my thirst in dew drops and whet my ap-
petite."

XIII.

Seek out Szegedin's Csarda's sign,
And whilst the hostess brings the wine,
See *Barna Bandi** at his ease,
With charger tethered near 'midst trees.

"God bless all here," and when drunk up
He bids his neighbor taste the cup;
He cocks his round hat o'er his ear
As *Barna Bandi's* song rings clear.

"From Theiss's strand black clouds swift move,
When Barna Bandi weeps his love;
Beneath the limbs of giant oak
Brown Andres' smothered tears do choke."

"Weep not thy sweetheart's fickle mind,
For many just as good you'll find!
Our dark-skinned maids will make amend,
Forget her; heaven another'll send."

He speaks no word, gulps down his woe,
His raven eyes with tear-drops glow!
He drains his glass—his steed bestrides,
And like the storm to Puszta rides!

---

* Brown Andres.

XIV.

Pretty Ilona. Good morning, Judge, good morning,
   You're early up to day !
Judge. What brings thee here, Ilona,
   So early out this way ?
Pretty Ilona. My geese I drove, as usual,
   To pasture on rich grass,
  The judge's son sprang on them
   And drove them down the pass ;
  The judge's son hath ruined
   My whole goosedom, alas !
Judge. Say then, what shall I pay thee,
   For all these stately geese ?
Pretty Ilona. Sir Judge, you must be noble,
   And give me back my peace.
  For every downy feather
   A coin of purest gold,
  For every slender anklet
   A spoon of gilded mould,
  For every weakly winglet
   A burnished golden plate,
  For every silvery throatlet
   A golden trumpet's weight.
Judge. Your wishes, sweet Ilona, are
   Too dear a price for me,
  The judge's youthful son may hang
   Upon the gallows-tree.

Pretty Ilona. A bargain ! . . . But with rosebuds sweet
　　　His gallows shall I deck !
　　　My tender arms shall be the noose
　　　That winds about his neck !

XV.

Tell me, comrade, why my sack-
Sleeves are closed and buttoned back ?
In one tinder, steel and stone,
In the other bank notes are sewn.

If the Puszta fails to please
Csarda surely'll give me ease ;
Hostess waits upon my wink,
Brings the guest her best to drink.

Still they envy me and say
That on honest folks I prey ;
Dickens seize them—I ne'er speak !
He who drinks not must grow weak.

XVI.

I'm a laddie, poor and deft,
Daily bread I earn by theft ;
Should my heart from stealing bend
Then my life would surely end.

If I cease my pilfering trade
Still I'm called a filching blade;
So I'll keep my robber's name
Striving to deserve the fame.

If I fill my glass or not
Still they call me " drunken sot ;"
So I'll keep my tippler's name,
Striving to deserve the fame.

XVII.

Seated in their spin-room high
Maidens weep, as shuttles fly ;
" Mother, quickly help impart,
Spinning weareth out our heart."

" Pretty shoes I'll give, for peace,
If your crying you will cease."
" Mother, quickly help impart,
'Tis not shoes that grieve our heart."

" Handsome gowns shall you array,
If you'll dry your tears away."
" Mother, quickly help impart,
'Tis not gowns that grieve our heart."

" See, I'll bring you tender beaux,
If you'll end your wailing woes."

" Mother, now you help impart,
Lack of lovers wrings our heart."

XVIII.

I'm a widow's girl; my feet
    Like pure snow are bright;
He who doubts my word may look—
    I'll give him the right.

I'm my mother's child; my rosy
    Lips o'er pearls unite;
He who doubts my word may kiss—
    I'll give him the right.

XIX.

Sultry heats are on us now,
Soon there'll come a change, I trow;
From the rose, dear to my heart,
Soon must I in grief depart.

Now my rosebud's gone away,
Gone in stranger-lands to stray,
Left for me a message true
That his steps I should pursue.

Would that I but knew the street,
Where he placed his weary feet,

With a golden plough I'd trace
Furrows o'er its precious face!

And the seeds that there I'd sow
Should be pearls of purest glow,
And to moisten their earth-bed
Many a tear my eyes should shed.

All around with grief I'd weep,
Hang up cloths of mourning deep;
At the day-dawn, black as night,
At the sun-set, snowy white.

XX.

Hath the night turned to red day?
Must my precious flee away?
    My jewel, yet stay,
    A little delay,
Sweetest flower, my voice obey.

Sinks the sun at dim twilight,
Wilt thou come to-morrow night?
    Thou, my life,
    My longing, strife,
All the world to me, dear wight!

XXI.

The meads must ripen 'neath the blaze
Of all-consuming sunbeams' rays;
Alas, my beauty burns away,
A-withered, pained, from heart-decay !

The fields at last are ripened o'er,
The farmer garners up his store;
For my o'er-ripe and wearied breath
My only harvester is—Death.

TRANSYLVANIAN ROUMANIAN
VOLK-SONGS.

VOLK-SONGS OF THE TRANSYLVANIAN ROUMANIANS.

I.

I roamed of late the woods along,
As green as May, and full of song;
Now when my steps press the same way,
'Tis mute and withered, ashen gray.

Oh forest brave! oh lofty trees!
Spread thy cool shadows to the breeze;
That cushioned in thy mossy bed
My lap may hold my darling's head!

(A. C. L. V., III. 118, 1378.)

II.

Heather flower, it cannot be
That she's broke her trist with me;
In the darkness hath she strayed,
And I've lost my darling maid,
While my life must forfeit be.

(A. C. L. V., I. 18, 934.)

III.

Flirting maiden, this for thee
Shall my wish of wishes be;
On thy door-sill, hour by hour,
Shalt thou shiver, crouch and cower;
Like a taper, all on fire,
Shalt thou burn and ne'er expire;
When the midnight hour outtones
Death-cold sweat shall rend thy bones;
When the night gives place to day
Icy frost shall bear thee 'way.

(*A. C. L. V., I. 50, 966.*)

IV.

Weeping willow, green of leaf,
My sweetheart hath wrought me grief,
Folds another to her breast—
Yet this troubles not my rest.
But one thing doth on me prey
That I said to her one day,
" Dearest, I will kisses give,
Nor forget thee whilst I live."

(*A. C. L. V., I. 81, 997.*)

V.

Why direct thy saddened mien
To yon lofty rock-ravine?

Look, what near before thee lies,
To the vineyard raise thine eyes,
See, a wagon rolls away,
Full of human freight to-day !
Climb the appletree—your beau
Down the mountain-path doth go ;
Little is his garment worn,
But his heart hath long been torn.

(A. C. L. V., I. 82, 998.)

VI.

Come to me, thou rosebud brave,
All that's sweet in life shalt have ;
Never shalt thou shoeless go,
Save alone thou'd have it so,
Gladly would I see each toe ;
To the mill-wheel ne'er shall corn
On thy burdened back be borne ;
Yet unless thou bear'st the sack
Shall thy stomach fodder lack.

(A. C. L. V., III. 86, 1345.)

VII.

Swallow, little birdie free,
Will'st a message bear for me ?
Take this note to far-off land,
Drop it in my sweetheart's hand ;
Should she ask from whence you came,
Should she seek the writer's name,

Say—the one from whom I've flown,
Loves thee, darling, thee alone.

(*A. C. L. V., III. 87, 1346.*)

VIII.

Poor old Gypsey man am I,
Parents both are long since dead,
For my griefs there's none will cry
Though my gaze o'er all hath sped.
In the heaven the stars I trace,
On the earth no friendly face,
No one pitieth my sad lot—
God alone hath not forgot.

(*A. C. L. V., V. 16, 1588.*)

IX.

Dearest love in stranger land,
Send a tiding quick to hand ;
Through the post or through the sun
And my life in pleasure'll run ;
Through the post, or through a star,
For I languish while thou'rt far ;
And my raven locks each day
Leave my head and fall away ;
Though each tress with butter pure
I anoint to keep it sure,
Of no use e'en honey-comb—
Dearest, will't thou ne'er come home !

(*A. C. L. V., VI. 14, 1880.*)

TRANSYLVANIAN ZIEGEUNER
VOLK-SONGS.

VOLK-SONGS OF THE TRANSYLVANIAN ZIEGEUNER.

I.

Kiss me, dearest darling mine,
And I'll buy a ribbon fine;
Let me nestle on thy arm,
And I'll buy a Mentè * warm;
Should'st thou play a faithless trick,
Then I'll get a cudgel thick.

II.

Crush no flowret in thy way,
List to what its petals say;
Let me dwell in spring-time mild,
None shield me from north winds wild,
Like thee, I'm a Gypsey child.

III.

Spruce young fellow, fair of face,
'Round thy cap sweet flowers place,
Yet for all the buds you wear
Sure your senses are not there.

*The fur mantle worn in the Hungarian National costume.

IV.

Tender maiden, free from care,
Like a ducat, fresh and fair;
Withered spinster, haggard wife,
Like a weed 'midst meadow life.

V.

In the wood and in the tree
Sings the birdie when he's free;
'Neath the mother's watchful care
Lives the maid most free from snare.

VI.

Soon will Christmas day be here,
Scarce is wood, and bad and dear;
Heaven end the serf's despite!
Send him wood, and bread so white.

VII.

Thou, oh God, hast decked the earth
With flowery meads and joy and mirth,
Hast sent the cheering sunbeam's ray,
And hast ordained the Easter-day;
I pray thee, God, my cot inspect,
My table's with fresh linen decked.

VIII.

In the wood a glee bird sings,
Joyful Gypsey laddie springs ;
When Whitsuntide comes again,
All forgot is winter pain.

IX.

In flowery meads seek roses rare,
And kisses from thy Lizzie fair ;
Then sing and dance with frolic fire
Before thy dear one's aged sire ;
And if his liquor mounts above
Take speedy care to tell thy love.

$$(A.\ C.\ L.\ V.,\ l.\ \tfrac{116}{1032})$$

X.

Ne'er a father's care I've known,
Poor in friends I roam alone,
Long since is my mother dead,
Sweetheart starved for lack of bread;
Thou alone, my fiddle's song,
Through the world with me dost throng.

$$(A.\ C.\ L.\ V.,\ l.\ \tfrac{116}{1032})$$

XI.

Forge the iron, strike with might,
Like a true-born Gypsey smite ;

Yet for all, be ever poor,
Full of woe, my heart and sore;
Yet should I win a precious aim,
Could I within this glowing flame
My darling's heart till tender smite,
No man was e'er so rich a wight.

(*A. C. L. V., II.* $\frac{127}{1307}$)

XII.

Beauteous is the maiden fair,
Bright her silken robes, and rare;
But a Gypsey-girl's for me
Far a sweeter sight to see.
In the grass she'll lie so still,
Pet and kiss me all I will.

(*A. C. L. V., II.* $\frac{112}{1172}$)

XIII.

Maid, thy love hath proved my curse,
Stripped me e'en of shirt and purse!
God shall singe thy heart with pain,
Then my own will burst in twain.

(*A. C. L. V., II.* $\frac{112}{1175}$)

XIV.

He's a jolly chap, my beau,
Sure none others like him grow;

In town gray or in fields green,
No one like him can be seen.
When his bow the strings doth sweep,
Great and little, all, must weep ;
If throughout the world you go
There's none other like him—no !

(*A. C. L. V.*, *II.* $\frac{93}{1175}$)

XV.

Since the hour I saw the light
Twenty years have ta'en their flight ;
Twice ten years of torture slow,
Scanty pleasure, plenty woe.

(*A. C. L. V.*, *II.* $\frac{94}{1176}$)

XVI.

From the moment I was born
No one cared for me forlorn,
In the damp grass have I lain,
'Till for baptism fell the rain.

(*A. C. L. V.*, *III.* $\frac{23}{1278}$)

XVII.

God of mercy, tell, I crave,
How my soul to surely save !
Shall my God forgotten be,
While I rob and wassail free ?

Had I but three happy days, ·
Then in peace I'd mend my ways.

(A. C. L. V., IV. $\frac{16}{1530}$)

XVIII.

My wife's mother's drunk again,
Now, for once, I'll peace obtain ;
Heaven bless her host, I say,
O'er him may no trouble stray!
Should she only soggy be
Like another dame is she;
Silence, gently, all keep still—
And I'll do just what I will!

(A. C. L. V., III. $\frac{22}{1278}$)

XIX.

Now Bonschida's far from here,
And my sweetheart's far, I fear ;
I must lie in lengthened pain
'Till I see her once again,
Then I'll kiss her mouth so white
While her arms enfold me tight.

(A. C. L. V.,III. $\frac{15}{2513}$)

XX.

Whither blows the roaring wind?
From the churchyard comes its breath,
Deep I grieve my father's death.

Whither blows the roaring wind?
From the forest sweeps the blast,
Deep I grieve my mother past.

Whither blows the roaring wind?
From the highway is it borne,
Deeply I my brother mourn.

Whither blows the roaring wind?
From the ravine's fearsome head,
Deep I grieve my sister dead.